The Girls of the Good Day Orphanage

❧ Good ❧
Charlotte

by CAROL BEACH YORK

illustrated by Victoria de Larrea

cover illustration by John Speirs

D0616069

A
LITTLE APPLE
PAPERBACK

SCHOLASTIC INC.

New York   Toronto   London   Auckland   Sydney

ISBN 0-590-40845-3

12 11 10 9 8 7 6 5 4 3 2 1   2   4 5 6 7 8 9/9

Printed in the U.S.A.   40

This story is affectionately dedicated to
AGNES ERICKSON

Mrs. Singlittle Takes Charge

It was a dark and gloomy day. All the old brick houses around Butterfield Square seemed to be hunched and huddled in the cold and misty rain. The streets were deserted. No one was out on such a day. Even the trees looked forlorn. All afternoon the rain fell, wetting the sidewalks and black iron fences, trickling down the windowpanes, spattering against the sign at Number 18: THE GOOD DAY ORPHANAGE FOR GIRLS.

Inside The Good Day a fire burned in the parlor fireplace, and some very good smells were coming from the kitchen where Cook was baking pumpkin pies and macaroni.

But the cozy fireside and warm kitchen were deserted. Everyone was in the large front hallway: Cook in her apron; all the twenty-eight Good Day girls in their blue dresses and white collars, black shoes, and long black stockings; Miss Lavender and Miss Plum, the ladies who took care of the girls; and a large, round-faced woman whose name was Mrs. Singlittle.

The hall was crowded, and the noise was tremendous with all twenty-eight little girls hopping about and talking at once. But no one said to the girls, "Hush now, we must be quiet." For an unexpected thing was happening — something that had never happened before.

Miss Lavender and Miss Plum were going away for a whole two weeks' vacation. They were going together, and that was what had never happened before.

Miss Plum's nephew Reginald was going to be married, and Miss Lavender and Miss Plum were traveling on a train to go to the wedding. Their suitcases were full of nice things to eat while they traveled, and books to read, and presents wrapped in tissue paper for all of Miss Plum's relatives. And there was one especially large package with a bow as big as a cabbage: That was the wedding present. It was a silver dish so shiny that you could see your face in it. All the girls had watched as Miss Lavender wrapped up the dish and Miss Plum tied on the big ribbon.

The girls wished they were going to see Reginald and all of Miss Plum's relatives and the wedding. But, still, it was exciting to be left behind without either Miss Lavender or Miss Plum.

Mrs. Singlittle opened the front door and stuck her large ruddy face into the rain and mist. "What a dismal day," she announced, as though the others might not have noticed. Mrs. Singlittle was going to take care of the girls while Miss Lavender and Miss Plum were away. She was full of energy and eager to begin.

Miss Lavender was so flustered and excited that she could not seem to find anything she needed.

"Where is my glove?" she asked. "My left

glove is gone!" After finding her left glove, and her handbag, and her umbrella, she almost left without her suitcase.

Miss Plum was a good deal calmer, and she had her gloves and handbag and umbrella well under control. She stood straight and serene, as tall and thin as Miss Lavender was short and plump. Miss Plum kissed each one of the twenty-eight little girls good-bye with a special word for each:

"Now, Little Ann, stay out of Cook's way; Elsie May, you are oldest and you must help Mrs. Singlittle; good-bye, Nonnie, remember to practice your piano every day; Phoebe, I hope to see that your toothbrush chart is full of checks when I return. . . ."

On she went, saying something special to everyone . . . until she reached the very last of all. Miss Plum could not help smiling as she pushed the dark hair back from the last little girl's forehead. Large dark eyes stared up at Miss Plum from under the hair.

"Good-bye, Tatty — " Miss Plum paused. There were so many instructions she should give to Tatty. Where could she begin? Don't forget to make your bed . . . don't forget to wash your hands before meals . . . try to keep your hair combed and your stockings pulled up and your dress clean . . . study your spelling words and sit up straight at the table and don't lose your mittens. . . . Where to begin indeed? At last Miss Plum only kissed Tatty and said, "We'll be thinking about you."

"Here comes your taxicab," Mrs. Singlittle cried as a yellow car appeared through the rain, a solitary sight upon the deserted street.

Out went Miss Lavender and Miss Plum, their umbrellas opened. Elsie May and two other girls followed behind carrying the suitcases. When Miss Plum and Miss Lavender were all tucked away in the taxicab, the girls ran back to the house. They watched with the others as the cab went away through the rain and was soon out of sight.

No one knew it, but a small gold pin in the shape of a butterfly had fallen from Miss Lavender's coat (probably not fastened securely by Miss Lavender in her excitement). The pin lay at the edge of the walk by the gate, splashed with raindrops, but no one noticed.

"Good-bye, good-bye," the girls called one last time as Mrs. Singlittle closed the door.

It seemed very quiet in the hall, after all the bustle and hubbub of Miss Plum and Miss Lavender's getting ready to go.

"Well," said Cook, clearing her throat and sniffing, "I guess I'll get back to my pies —"

The girls stood about aimlessly, feeling rather shy and strange to be left alone with Mrs. Singlittle.

Mrs. Singlittle seemed to be the only one who was not at a loss for something to do. "Come along, girls," she said. "We are going to get acquainted." She clapped her hands and all her rings flashed in the lamplight. "Follow me." And she led the way into the parlor.

Only Tatty did not hear. She had drawn aside one of the lace curtains at the long thin window beside the door and was looking far off down the square into the rain. Already she had begun to miss Miss Lavender and Miss Plum.

Good Charlotte

The next thing Tatty knew, the hall was quiet and empty. No one was there except herself. From the parlor she could hear Mrs. Singlittle's voice:

"Now we have time to get acquainted before supper."

As though a thunderbolt had struck her, Tatty remembered where she was and what she was supposed to be doing. She scurried as fast as she could go toward the parlor door. Miss Lavender and Miss Plum had not been gone two minutes, Tatty thought, and already she was in trouble. She hesitated at the parlor door and was just stepping in timidly when Mrs. Singlittle said, "Will someone close that door, please?"

Mrs. Singlittle had her back to the parlor door as she spoke. Tatty closed the door as she stepped in, and just at that moment Mrs. Singlittle turned. Her face lighted with pleasure to see her request obeyed so promptly.

"Ah, there's a good girl," Mrs. Singlittle said. She beckoned Tatty to come to her. Tatty went obediently, wishing she had remembered to pull up her stockings and find her hair ribbon.

"What is *your* name?" asked Mrs. Singlittle.

"Tatty," the little girl answered.

"Tatty?" Mrs. Singlittle cocked her head to one side to decide what she thought of that. Then she bent down.

"Tatty," she said again. "What kind of a name is that?"

"It's short for Charlotte," Tatty said. She was fascinated by the smell of perfume and the sight of Mrs. Singlittle's plump pink face coming closer and closer to her.

"*Charlotte!*" Mrs. Singlittle exclaimed, and everyone jumped.

"Charlotte," she said a second time, only a little less loudly. "That's one of the most beautiful names in the world."

Tatty stared at Mrs. Singlittle. No one had ever told her that.

"Much too pretty not to use," Mrs. Singlittle declared. "Tatty, indeed. While *I* am here, *I* would like to call you Charlotte. Would that be all right?"

Tatty nodded. Then she noticed the tiny gold earrings that hung on thin gold wires

from Mrs. Singlittle's pierced ears. She had never seen earrings like that before.

"Of course it will be all right," Mrs. Singlittle echoed heartily. "Such a good girl—my good Charlotte." Then she gave Tatty a hug and a kiss. She did not notice that some of the other girls were beginning to giggle and nudge each other.

But Tatty noticed. She saw the girls giggling and whispering and looking over at her. "Good Charlotte!" Elsie May said in a loud mocking whisper. The girls laughed more than ever.

Tatty hung her head miserably. The girls were right. How long could Mrs. Singlittle go on calling her *good* Charlotte? Tatty, who was last to the table at mealtimes, who chewed her pencils and got holes in the knees of her stockings. . . . How long before Mrs. Singlittle would realize her mistake?

The Girl with the Blue Hair

After Mrs. Singlittle had introduced herself to each of the twenty-eight girls, she chose three girls to shell nuts for Cook.

First Mrs. Singlittle chose Elsie May, who was the biggest girl of all. She was rather vain because she had beautiful yellow braids tied with fancy bows.

Then Mrs. Singlittle chose Mary. Mary had red hair and three hundred and eleven freckles (a visitor named Miss Know It All had told her so).

And Mrs. Singlittle chose Tatty.

"You, too, my good Charlotte," Mrs. Singlittle said.

She gave the girls three nutcrackers that Cook had managed to find in the kitchen drawers. Then she said, "You may sit here by the fireplace and be out of Cook's way."

Left alone in the cozy parlor, the three girls sat in a semicircle before the fire. There were three bowls lined up along the hearth: a bowl of nuts—pecans with thin red shells and almonds with rough white shells and walnuts; an empty bowl to put the shells in; and a small bowl for the nutmeats.

"Try to be careful and don't crush the walnut shells," said Elsie May, taking charge. "We can make things out of them."

"What things?" asked Tatty. She had not thought of crushing a walnut shell. The big walnuts were too hard for her even to crack.

"Oh, things," said Elsie May as though Tatty was too little to understand.

"Pin holders, she means," Mary said.

"And we can paint them and make ornaments."

"Oh," said Tatty. She was struggling with a pecan, which kept slipping out of her nutcracker and bouncing on the carpet. She was afraid Mrs. Singlittle was going to be very disappointed in her because she could not crack nuts very well. In fact, it seemed she could not crack them at all.

Mary liked to crack her nuts as hard as she could and watch the shells fly.

"You're getting shells all over," Elsie May scolded.

"So are you," Mary answered, which was true. It was hard to crack nuts without scattering a few pieces of nutshell, even if you were very careful.

Tatty was still struggling with her first pecan when Mrs. Singlittle came back into the parlor. She smiled over at the girls and said, "That's my good Charlotte—I see you're not getting shells all over the rug."

"She can't get shells all over if she can't

even crack a nut," Elsie May muttered under her breath. But Mrs. Singlittle had bustled out again and did not hear. Tatty finally did get a nut cracked open, but by that time she was so hungry she ate it.

"Don't eat all the nuts," said Elsie May.

They were nearly finished with their job when two other girls came into the parlor. Phoebe, who was pretending to be a wild lion, crawled on her hands and knees and shook her soft brown hair fiercely. Little Ann, the very smallest girl at The Good Day, was riding on the wild lion and shrieking with laughter.

Round and round the room clumped Phoebe; louder and louder laughed Little Ann. And then suddenly all five girls became aware that someone was standing in the parlor doorway. They looked and saw a strange girl wearing a brown coat and hood. They had never seen her before.

Phoebe sat up on her knees, and Little Ann tumbled off to the floor behind her.

Elsie May and Mary and Tatty looked over their shoulders from their circle by the fire.

"Excuse me," said the strange girl in a very gentle voice, "I guess no one heard me knock. I was just going by and I saw this by your gate outside. I thought it must belong to someone who lives here."

She opened her hand, and there lay Miss Lavender's gold butterfly pin, still wet in spots, but as shiny as ever and not damaged at all by the rain. The girl stepped closer to the fireplace and held out the pin.

"Why, it's Miss Lavender's butterfly," said Elsie May. "Here—I'll take it. Miss Lavender is away now."

As the girl laid the gold pin in Elsie May's hand, the hood of her coat slipped back and all the other girls gasped. The strange girl had blue hair. Long and silky and blue as a summer sky.

The girls did not know what to think. Then they also noticed that she did not

have ordinary shoes on her feet. Her shoes were white satin with tiny pearls sewed on and heels made of gold.

As they all stared, Elsie May was the first to speak. "You've dyed your hair!" she exclaimed.

The visitor smiled when she heard this. "Oh, no, I didn't dye my hair at all," she said. She looked at Elsie May curiously to see what other funny things Elsie May would say. Phoebe began to giggle.

Elsie May did not have anything more to say for the moment, so the strange girl began to look around from face to face and stopped at last at Tatty's.

"Excuse me," she said softly, "but are you eight years old?"

"Almost," said Tatty. Her eyes were wide as she stared at this odd little girl who had appeared so unexpectedly in their parlor.

"I'm eight," the girl said to Tatty. "Can't we be friends?" Then she looked around at the others hopefully. "Can't we all be friends?" She even looked at Elsie May, but Elsie May was not sure she wanted to be friends with anyone so peculiar as a girl with blue hair—even if she did have satin shoes.

"I'm twelve," said Elsie May in such a way that the stranger would see she was the one in charge. She put Miss Lavender's butterfly pin on the mantelpiece and sat down again by the fire.

"I'm nine," said Mary.

"I'm ten," said Phoebe.

"I'm five," said Little Ann. Little Ann thought that blue hair and satin shoes were beautiful. She wished she had them both. "What's your name?" she asked shyly.

"My name is Esmerelda," said the girl. "I'm an enchanted princess."

"Ooooffff!" shrieked Elsie May. "An enchanted princess! Hhhhaaaa!"

"It's true, I'm afraid," said Esmerelda, "and it may be funny for you, but it's not very funny for me. I wish I were home in my castle."

Mary began to laugh now, too, rolling her eyes at Elsie May. Phoebe shook her head and roared like a lion. Tatty and Little Ann were not sure whether to laugh or not. They just stared at Esmerelda, with her long, shiny blue hair and her white satin shoes with gold heels.

"Do you really live in a castle?" Tatty asked at last.

"Yes, I really do," said Esmerelda.

"Oh, what lies!" cried Elsie May.

"I *do* live in a castle," Esmerelda insisted gently. Her face was very sad. "You believe me, don't you?" she said to Tatty.

"I—I guess so," said Tatty, not very loudly.

"You believe me, don't you?" Esmerelda said to Little Ann. But Little Ann only stared back at her with wide eyes.

"How did you get enchanted?" Mary asked.

Just then several other girls who had been helping Cook in the kitchen came down the hall. As they passed the parlor door they saw the girl with blue hair, and they hurried into the parlor asking: "Who's this?" "What's happening?"

"*Ssshhh*," said Mary. "This is Esmerelda, an enchanted princess, and she's going to tell us how she got enchanted."

"Oh, what lies," Elsie May said again, and closed her eyes.

"The goblins enchanted me," Esmerelda said, as the newcomers sat down on the floor in front of the fire. Esmerelda sat on a footstool and clasped her hands around her knees. The firelight flickered on her face and on her blue hair and satin shoes.

"I'm really not a little girl at all. I'm a grown-up princess. I really do live in a lovely castle, and someday I will marry a handsome prince."

"Didn't anyone ever tell you it's wrong to tell lies?" asked Elsie May. But all the other girls said, "*Ssshhh*." They wanted to

hear Esmerelda's story, even if it was
made up.

"Why did the goblins enchant you?"
Mary asked. "Did you do something bad?"

"Did you forget to wash your hands
before supper?" asked Little Ann.

"Did you leave your vegetables?"
another girl asked.

"Did you lose your mittens?" asked
another.

"Did you run in the house?"

"Did you get mud on your shoes?"

"Did you break a good dish?"

"No, no, no." Esmerelda kept shaking
her head at every question. "I didn't do
any of those things. All I did was walk in

the goblins' part of the forest. They don't like anyone to do that. I just didn't realize how far I had walked, and all of a sudden there I was by the bramble-bushes, and out jumped all the goblins, and before I could run away they made a circle around me."

"Then what happened?" whispered Little Ann, moving closer to Tatty.

"The goblins began to cry, 'Enchant her, enchant her.' And Old Goblin—she's the leader—began to rub her scratchy old fingers together." Esmerelda rubbed her own fingers to show the girls how Old Goblin had done it. "Old Goblin was so excited to have me trapped she hardly knew where to begin. Nobody ever goes into the goblins' part of the forest because the goblins are so wicked, so they don't have many chances to enchant people.

" 'Make her into a little girl,' one of the goblins suggested. I guess she thought that was a terrible punishment. 'Ahhhhhh,' Old Goblin agreed, and chanted:

'A little girl with blue hair
Eight years in all,
A little girl far from home
Till the first snowfall.' "

"What does that mean?" Mary asked.

"It means I cannot go home and I must stay enchanted until the first snow falls," Esmerelda said.

"Ohhh," sighed Elsie May, "such dreadful, dreadful lies." She closed her eyes again as though she could not even bear to think about it all.

But the other girls paid no attention to Elsie May. "Go on, go on," they said to Esmerelda.

So Esmerelda continued.

"I said to the goblins, 'Please don't enchant me. I don't want to be a little girl with blue hair. I want to be myself, Princess Esmerelda, and I want to go home to my castle.' But the goblins only laughed. Finally one of them said, 'Let's let her keep her own shoes.' All of a sudden I looked down at myself, and there I was, a little girl with this dress and coat and hood. Only my own shoes were left."

"What were your real clothes like?" Phoebe asked.

"I was wearing a long pink dress embroidered with roses of gold thread. And I was wearing my second-best crown. And my diamond rings and bracelets, too, for I always wear them."

"Oh, oh, oh," chanted Elsie May, shaking her head. "Oh, oh, oh."

"Then what happened?" asked Tatty.

"Well, there I was—only my shoes left of the real me," said Esmerelda. "Then one of the goblins said, 'Let her have three wishes.' I was about to say 'Good! I wish myself unenchanted,' but the goblin added: 'Three wishes that she may *not* use to break the enchantment.'

" 'All right,' the other goblins agreed, and Old Goblin leaned down close to me —awful she is, with two warts on her nose and a long hair growing out of each—and she said, 'Until the first snow falls, Princess Esmerelda—hey, hey, hey—until the first snow falls.'

"And the next thing I knew I was walking down a street in the rain, your street. I wished the rain would turn to snow. But that didn't work, of course, because it would have ended the enchantment. So then I wished the rain would stop—and the rain stopped."

"Oh, sure," Elsie May said with a hoot.

"But the rain *has* stopped!" Some of the girls had run to the window and pulled aside the curtain to look out. At last, after all that long, cold, dreary, wet day, the rain had stopped. A woman walking along the street carried her closed-up-tight umbrella under her arm.

Everyone was very quiet for a moment, and Little Ann snuggled closer to Tatty. She was thinking about Old Goblin with her warts.

"Then I saw the golden pin lying by your gate," Esmerelda continued, "and I brought it in. No one heard me knock, so I just opened the door and came in. And here I am," she added sadly, "until the first snow comes. I hope it will be soon." She sighed and looked around at the circle of faces.

"Did you ever hear such a story in your life?" Elsie May said. She stood up and brushed a few tiny pieces of nutshell from her skirt.

"Yes, it's just a made-up story," the other girls began to say. Only Tatty and Little Ann were quiet.

But at last, because Esmerelda looked so sad and lonely, Tatty heard herself saying, "I will be your friend."

The other girls stared at Tatty, surprised to think she believed all the crazy things this strange girl said.

As the girls stood around in amazement, Tatty heard a knock at the door. Oh, dear, she thought, what more could happen in only one afternoon?

Mr. Not So Much

What more could happen was clear at once. Mr. Not So Much arrived at just that moment at the door of Number 18 Butterfield Square. He was grim and forbidding, dressed all in black.

His knock at the door was answered by Mrs. Singlittle herself. The girls in the parlor were so busy talking to the girl with the blue hair that—except for Tatty—they did not hear Mr. Not So

Much knock. The first thing they heard was his familiar voice in the hallway.

"Yes, the rain has stopped at last," Mr. Not So Much was saying.

"This time of year one really expects snow more than rain," Mrs. Singlittle answered.

At the sound of Mr. Not So Much's voice, the girls in the parlor stared at one another fearfully. They shrank back and tried to make themselves look small so Mr. Not So Much would not notice them when he came into the room.

"It's Mr. Not So Much," Elsie May whispered. "Just wait till he sees *you*," she said to Esmerelda.

Esmerelda looked frightened. It seemed that she was just barely away from the goblins, and now here she was about to meet someone *else* dreadful.

"What will he do to me?" she asked.

"Probably eat you up," said Elsie May, and the other girls looked horrified at her answer.

They could hear Mr. Not So Much coming down the hall toward the parlor, and all the girls looked at Tatty. She had said she would be Esmerelda's friend, and they were wondering what she would do now. Tatty looked around desperately for someplace to hide Esmerelda.

"Here—back here—" she said, pushing the poor enchanted princess into the first place she could think of: behind the parlor curtains. Not a moment too soon! Mr. Not So Much appeared at that instant in the parlor doorway, glooming and frowning and snapping his gloves against his palm.

"Well, well, what's all this, what's all this?" He stared around at the frightened faces of the girls. "Miss Plum and Miss Lavender hardly on their way and already you have nothing to do?"

Mrs. Singlittle came right along behind Mr. Not So Much, and she quickly said, "The girls are cracking nuts for Cook. I've put them straight to work, you see."

"All these girls?" Mr. Not So Much

looked very upset to see what appeared to be nearly half The Good Day assigned to cracking nuts.

"Well..." Mrs. Singlittle looked rather surprised herself to see that her three girls had grown to three times that number. But before she could say anything else, Mr. Not So Much began stalking around the parlor in his usual way.

"Not so much wood on the fire," he said. "Not so much electricity burning."

Mr. Not So Much was a director on the board of directors of The Good Day. He came once a month to see how things were going, and he always found things going very badly, or so it seemed to him.

He found too much noise, and too much confusion, and too much chatter.

But worst of all he found *too much money being spent*. He found cakes heaped with frosting and muffins stuffed with raisins. He found too much shoe polish being used and too much starch, and

too much money being spent on hair ribbons and toothpaste and shampoo.

In the summertime he found the front walk full of roller skates and the refrigerator full of popsicles. In the wintertime he found fires full of burning wood and Christmas trees full of tinsel. And in every season he found twenty-eight little girls growing rapidly out of their clothes.

Every time he came, Mr. Not So Much tried to explain the need for economy and thrift to Miss Plum and Miss Lavender. They did not seem to understand. (They only listened and nodded and smiled, and were happy when he left at last.)

Miss Plum and Miss Lavender had warned Mrs. Singlittle that Mr. Not So Much would be coming that afternoon to check up on things, but they could not have prepared her for what he was now about to say. Planting his feet firmly on the carpet, clasping his hands behind his back, and glowering around at everyone, he announced:

"Now that Miss Plum and Miss Lavender are away, I think it would be best if I stop in every day until they come back."

All the girls gulped and trembled and stared back at Mr. Not So Much. This was more horrible than they could have dreamed. What would they do with Mr. Not So Much tramping about every day!

Then, addressing himself to Mrs. Singlittle, Mr. Not So Much continued: "You have no idea of the amount of managing needed here. Wasteful ways must be stopped. A penny saved is a penny earned. There are ways to economize, Mrs. Singlittle, and I hope you will take advantage of them."

Mrs. Singlittle drew herself up grandly. Her earrings swayed on their tiny wires. "Mr. Not So Much," she said, like a brave soldier going into battle, "I will do my best."

Mr. Not So Much pulled on his lower lip and considered this. "That is what we must all try to do, Mrs. Singlittle—our very best."

He turned toward the girls to see that they were listening to this wise advice. However, their attention had been distracted by Esmerelda's satin shoes, sticking out quite plainly from under the bottom hem of the curtain. The girls began poking each other and motioning with their heads, until one by one they had all turned and seen the shoes sticking out. Now they didn't know what to do about it. Tatty reached out and tried to pull the curtain down over the shoes.

"Not so much fiddling there," Mr. Not So Much roared, and all the girls turned pale. Even Elsie May was too timid to speak up and tell on Esmerelda.

"That's my good Charlotte," Mrs. Singlittle said. "Trying to straighten that wrinkle in the curtain. Oh, she is such a good girl."

Mrs. Singlittle did not seem to see the satin shoes. Nor did Mr. Not So Much. The director scowled around one last time and then he said, "I will see you tomorrow, Mrs. Singlittle."

The little girls waited by the parlor fire. They heard Mr. Not So Much stomping away down the hall; they heard Mrs. Singlittle speak to him again by the door as he put on his coat and hat; they heard the door at last close after him.

But he was coming back again tomorrow. They would not be able to laugh or talk above a whisper, or play at anything that made any noise at all. Now they would not have nice warm fires burning. Or lovely cakes for dessert. Or anything nice. Now they would not have any fun at all.

Elsie May's Threat

The girls did not have long to brood and worry, for almost at once Mrs. Singlittle came back into the parlor.

Elsie May, full of courage now that Mr. Not So Much was gone, cried out, "Look who's here, Mrs. Singlittle!"

Elsie May pulled aside the curtain, and there stood Esmerelda with her blue hair and her satin shoes decorated with pearls. What was Mrs. Singlittle going to say to *that?* All the girls waited breathlessly.

Mrs. Singlittle only glanced toward Elsie May absently, and then she looked down at the three bowls by the fireplace.

"Look who's where?" she asked. "Come now, someone help me gather up these bowls. Cook will be pleased to see how many nuts you have cracked for her."

Tatty sprang forward quickly and picked up a bowl, hoping to distract Mrs. Singlittle's attention from Esmerelda.

"Ah, my good Charlotte," Mrs. Singlittle said. "My little helper."

"Look who's *here*, Mrs. Singlittle," Elsie May said again. This time she pulled poor Esmerelda forward so that Mrs. Singlittle could get a better look.

But Mrs. Singlittle only gazed rather blankly at Elsie May and asked again, "Look who is where, my dear?"

"Here, *here!*" Elsie May shook Esmerelda's arm fiercely. "This enchanted princess!"

Mrs. Singlittle smiled. "Oh, I see," she said, and she even went so far as to pat Elsie May's shoulder. "You're pretending you are an enchanted princess. That's nice, dear."

"I'm not pretending—*I'm* not pretending," Elsie May fairly shrieked, and the

other girls began to giggle. Mrs. Singlittle
did not even seem to see Esmerelda—
although how she could miss seeing someone with blue hair and satin shoes was
indeed a mystery.

"Don't shout so, dear," Mrs. Singlittle
said to Elsie May. "Can't you be quiet like
—like my good Charlotte here." Mrs.
Singlittle turned and drew Tatty toward
her and gave her a kiss. Elsie May's face
puffed up with rage. But Mrs. Singlittle
took all the bowls that Tatty had picked up
for her, put them one on top of the other,
and carried them out of the parlor toward
the kitchen. She didn't pay any more
attention to Elsie May.

When Mrs. Singlittle was gone, Esme-
relda pulled her arm away from Elsie
May and rubbed it with her fingers. Elsie
May had been tugging on it until it hurt.

"That lady didn't see me, you know,"
Esmerelda said to Elsie May. "I just remembered. No one who is over twelve
years old can see me. That was the last

thing the goblins added to the enchantment. Only children can see me."

"Why did the goblins do that?" asked
Mary, who was beginning to think Esmerelda might really be an enchanted
princess after all. Mrs. Singlittle had been
close enough to touch Esmerelda, but she
had not even seen her. It was as if she had
looked right through her. All the girls
drew closer now, a little less doubtful of
Esmerelda's story. Only Elsie May stood
frowning to herself.

"I guess the goblins thought it would be
harder for me if no grown-up could see
me," Esmerelda said. "I guess they
thought grown-ups would be helpful to
me, and they didn't think children could
do me much good."

"We can, too," all the girls began to say
at once. They did not like the goblins thinking that they could not be of any
help just because they weren't grown-up.

"We'll all be your friends," they said.
They began to touch Esmerelda's blue

hair. Little Ann got down on the floor and felt the beautiful satin shoes with her fingers. Esmerelda was really, truly, an enchanted princess, and they all knew it now.

"You won't even have to hide from Mr. Not So Much anymore," Phoebe said. "He's way over twelve."

How wonderful it would be to be invisible to Mr. Not So Much, they all thought.

"Just you wait, Tatty," Elsie May said at last. She was still angry because Mrs. Singlittle had said she should be quiet like Tatty, like "good Charlotte."

"I'll get even with you," said Elsie May.

And Tatty knew she meant it.

Stocking Feet

That night Esmerelda slept in Tatty's bed. It was a great honor for Tatty to have a real enchanted princess sleeping with her. Esmerelda chose Tatty because Tatty had been the very first one to say that she would be Esmerelda's friend. Esmerelda put her satin shoes under the bed right beside Tatty's slippers, and they snuggled down under the covers, whispering together until they fell asleep.

In the morning, when Tatty was getting dressed, she found that her school shoes were smeared inside with paste. She did not have to wonder long how that had happened—for Elsie May could not help poking her head in at the doorway (her hand over her mouth to hold back her giggles) to see how Tatty liked her sticky shoes.

"Oh, you!" said Tatty, when she saw Elsie May. She felt like throwing one of the shoes at Elsie May's head. But she was "good Charlotte" now, so instead she got a wet washcloth and tried to wash out the paste before it was time to go downstairs for breakfast. It was hard to be always good, she thought.

All the other girls in Tatty's room were ready. They were dressed and had made their beds and brushed their teeth and combed their hair. "Hurry up, Tatty," they said, and they rushed out of the bedroom and down the stairs.

"What about your breakfast?" Tatty said

to Esmerelda. Esmerelda was looking at her reflection in the mirror. She could not get used to the way she looked now that she was enchanted.

"Don't worry about me," she said to Tatty. "I'll just go down to the kitchen and have a snack there. Cook can't see me, you know."

"That's right, she can't," Tatty agreed. She thought that being invisible was not nearly as bad for Esmerelda as the goblins had thought it would be. I wish I were invisible, she thought miserably, staring down at her wet shoes. They were still

sticky in spots, although she had scrubbed and scrubbed.

Ahead lay a day of pitfalls. Mrs. Singlittle expected her to do everything right. Mr. Not So Much was coming. And Elsie May would probably be up to more mischief. Sighing, Tatty sat down on the floor and started to put on her shoes.

"Why don't you just carry your shoes along, until after breakfast," Esmerelda suggested. "They'll probably be all dry by then."

"That's a good idea," Tatty said, and she picked up a shoe in each hand. Then Esmerelda and Tatty hurried after the twenty-seven girls who had already gone down the stairs—and who had arrived with a great clackety-clatter in the dining room below.

"Oh, dear," said Mrs. Singlittle when she heard this. "What a commotion, what a commotion." She was not used to fifty-four feet clumping into a room at one time. Then, as the girls were taking their places at the long dining-room table, Mrs.

Singlittle caught sight of Tatty.

"Ah, there's my good Charlotte," she said. "Bless her heart, the only quiet one in the bunch. Good for you, Charlotte."

The other girls turned in their chairs to see Tatty come into the dining room with her shoes in her hands. Her black-stockinged feet did not make a sound on the polished floor.

"After this," said Mrs. Singlittle, "any girl who wants to has my permission to carry her shoes to breakfast for the next two weeks."

Well, of course, they all wanted to do that. It was not often that they got the chance to go around in their stocking feet. In fact, they *never* got the chance. They could hardly wait for tomorrow morning to come.

Then Tatty sat down at her place and found that she had no napkin and her spoon was on the floor under the table. As she got down to rescue the spoon, she saw Elsie May covering her mouth again to hold back her laughter.

Potato Soup (or: Mr. Not So Much in Cook's Kitchen)

After that, Tatty never knew what to expect—or when to expect it. All that day, Elsie May kept teasing Tatty and playing tricks on her. Tatty's shoes had no sooner dried from the paste than she found her hat was lost, and when she got to school and handed in her homework paper (a drawing of the sun and the moon), she found that Elsie May had written at the bottom: *"Hey diddle, diddle, the cat and the fiddle, the cow jumped over the moon."*

Tatty's teacher gave the drawing back to Tatty and said that a homework paper was not the place for foolishness.

"How do you expect to learn about the sun and the moon and our earth, if you are not concentrating?" the teacher asked.

Tatty was very ashamed to have everyone laugh at her paper. But when she got back to Butterfield Square there was no Miss Plum or Miss Lavender to comfort her, and Tatty was too timid to tell Mrs. Singlittle. Mrs. Singlittle was busy anyway, talking to Mr. Not So Much.

"Mr. Not So Much is here—*ssshhh*— Mr. Not So Much is here." The girls passed the word along as they came into the hall and heard his voice in the parlor. Tatty slipped in as quietly as she could with the other girls. They only wanted to hang up their coats and get away somewhere before Mr. Not So Much saw them. Tiptoeing to the long hall closet, they tried not to make a sound. Then someone dropped a book, and Mr. Not So Much came striding out of the parlor.

"Not so much noise," he said. "Not so much noise." Even Elsie May was speechless when Mr. Not So Much spoke. The only one who did not have to worry was Esmerelda. She had been sitting on the bottom step of the stairs in the hall, waiting for the girls to get back from school. Mr. Not So Much could not even see her.

The girls tried to be more quiet than ever hanging up their coats and hats, and Mr. Not So Much walked right past Esmerelda and out to the kitchen to see if good, economical, saving ways were in practice there.

Cook had been warned by Mrs. Singlittle that he was coming every single day while Miss Lavender and Miss Plum were gone. She had moved her cake and frosting supplies to the back of the cupboards. She had put her raisins and nuts and candied cherries in their tiny bottles at the back of the refrigerator. She had put a particularly delicious leftover plum cake into an empty pan and covered it with a lid.

When Mr. Not So Much came for his inspection, Cook was stirring a pot of potato soup.

"That's the way, that's the way." Mr. Not So Much rubbed his thin hands together and came as near to smiling as anyone had ever seen him. "A good, nourishing, substantial, economical meal. Nothing like potato soup."

Ugh, thought Cook. But she stirred away and smiled.

"What else is on the menu for dinner

tonight?" Mr. Not So Much asked. He looked around suspiciously for some sight of waste and extravagance and luxury beyond the capacity of The Good Day budget.

"Just a little brown bread," Cook said.

Mr. Not So Much narrowed his eyes. He was still suspicious, and at last Cook was forced to say, "Oh, yes—and this little cake for dessert." She produced from the cupboard a long, thin, flat cake, with no frosting. Mr. Not So Much picked it up and looked at it carefully from every angle. He really suspected that something rich and good and expensive was hidden somewhere about it; but he could find nothing wrong. It actually was a long, thin, flat, plain, unfrosted cake. Nothing wasteful there. Nothing extravagant.

"I see you have changed your ways," he said to Cook.

"Yes, sir," said Cook. "A penny saved is a penny earned."

"Those are my very thoughts exactly,"

Mr. Not So Much said triumphantly. He had been saying "A penny saved is a penny earned" to Miss Lavender and Miss Plum—and anyone else who would listen —for twenty years, since he had first become a director of The Good Day. After twenty years he was seeing some results at last.

With one final look around the bare kitchen, he left, and Cook went back to her potato soup. It was going to be a long, hard two weeks—she could see that.

When Will It Snow?

So there was the sad end to the first full day without Miss Lavender and Miss Plum. Potato soup and brown bread. To Tatty, after paste in her shoes and disgrace at school, it seemed a very poor day indeed. However, the dessert was not so bad. By the time the thin, flat, plain cake found its way to the dining room that night, each piece was covered with a scoop of peppermint ice cream.

Mrs. Singlittle was as happy to see this as the twenty-eight little girls were. She had been afraid she was not going to survive until morning on only a bowl of potato soup and a slice of brown bread.

"When do you think it will snow, Mrs. Singlittle?" Mary asked while they were eating their ice cream and cake. It certainly seemed cold enough to snow at any moment.

"Snow?" said Mrs. Singlittle. "Oh, yes, of course—snow. I suppose you're all eager to get out your sleds and make a snowman and things like that."

The twenty-eight girls looked around at each other, their eyes lowered, trying to hide their secret.

"Well, we may have snow tonight," Mrs. Singlittle said. "The weather report on the radio this afternoon said there was a possibility. And none too soon, I say. I should think we'd have had snow long before this."

Esmerelda went to the dining-room window and stared out into the darkness to see if she could see any snow falling. She was tired of being enchanted. She was tired of being a little girl with blue hair, eight years old—even with her own shoes, and even though she had found so many nice friends. There is no place like your own real true home, and Princess Esmerelda wanted hers.

But it did not snow that night. When the girls woke in the morning the streets were as bare as they had been the day before. The ground was frozen hard and the tree branches were stiff and black. There was not a speck of snow anywhere.

"Maybe it will snow today, or tonight," Tatty said, trying to cheer up Esmerelda.

"Oh, I suppose it will snow by and by," Esmerelda agreed wistfully. "You've never had a winter when there wasn't any snow at all, have you?" she asked suddenly, as an afterthought.

"Oh, no," said Tatty, "we've never had a winter without snow—yet."

They both looked out of the bedroom window wondering if this might, after all, turn out to be a winter without snow.

While they were looking through the

window, Phoebe came across the floor on her stomach, pretending she was swimming across the sea to China. All the beds were islands. The wall by the window was China. Phoebe could see the Chinese people standing there, but they did not see her, for their backs were turned. Phoebe rolled over and lay on her back to float and rest a while, and by squinting her eyes she could see the ceiling above as a white sky stretching over her ocean.

"Do you have snow where you live?" Tatty asked Esmerelda.

"Yes, we have snow and ice. Everything glistens. I have a long white coat all made of fur."

"Oh," said Tatty, sighing at the thought of having such a wonderful coat to wear.

Phoebe turned over on her stomach and swam the last few strokes to China. "What do you do all day in your castle?" she asked, rising from the ocean and sitting back on her heels.

"I stroll in the garden," said Esmerelda, "and eat cakes and honey. Sometimes I sit on my throne."

"Just like in the storybooks," said Phoebe with satisfaction. It must be marvelous to be a princess, she thought. And have a white coat all made of fur. And a throne. And a garden. And cakes with honey.

Phoebe began to swim back to her island, and Elsie May stuck her head in from the hallway. "You'll get your dress all wrinkled, Phoebe. Better get up, or I'll tell Mrs. Singlittle."

Phoebe made a face at Elsie May and hoisted herself up by her elbows onto her island bed. She was quite ready for breakfast now. Swimming to China took a lot of energy.

The Amazing Afternoon

That day Elsie May put salt in Tatty's spelling book. When Tatty opened the book at school all the salt trickled out across her desk, and the children sitting near her whispered and giggled. Down the aisle came the teacher, looking this way and that to see what was wrong. Tatty bent over her book and tried to look as if she were studying very hard. Little tears came into her eyes. She wished Miss Lavender and Miss Plum would come back.

Tatty missed three words on the spelling test, although she had studied as hard as she could until the very last minute. Even when the teacher was saying, "All right now, hand in your papers," Tatty was still mumbling to herself: "C-h-i-e-f, chief. Q-u-i-e-t, quiet." Still, she missed three words out of ten.

After school Tatty lagged behind the other girls, wondering what Mrs. Singlittle would think about such a poor spelling paper. Mary always got a hundred on her spelling papers, and so did Elizabeth, and Kate, and—well, just about everyone Tatty could think of.

Sadly she trudged along, staring down at her scuffed shoes and drooping stockings. She could not do anything right. She was not really "good Charlotte" at all, and everyone knew it. Mrs. Singlittle would know it, too, before the week was over. Then she would not hug Tatty and kiss her. Maybe she would say, "I am certainly disappointed in you, Charlotte." That was what the teacher said when Tatty missed her spelling words.

But when Tatty got to Number 18

Butterfield Square, Mrs. Singlittle did not ask to look at the spelling paper. She was not anywhere to be seen, and Tatty hung up her coat and hat and went out to the kitchen to see what Cook had for her. The other girls had already eaten their after-school snack and had gone up to their rooms or out into the back yard to play.

"Here you are, Tatty," said Cook. She gave Tatty a large round sugar cookie from the place where she was hiding cookies in the cupboard. (Mr. Not So Much had been around only an hour or so before, and Cook had once again swept her kitchen clean.)

Cook went out into the yard to talk to the handyman, and Tatty sat by the stove to eat her cookie. She had hardly begun when Elsie May came tiptoeing into the kitchen and helped herself to an extra cookie from the cupboard. She didn't care if Tatty saw. She knew Tatty wouldn't dare tell on her.

Elsie May was just starting out of the

kitchen when she heard Cook coming in at the back door. She knew Cook would scold her for taking an extra cookie without permission—and now she saw Mrs. Singlittle coming along the hall from the parlor. There was no place for Elsie May to go and no time for her to put back the stolen cookie. Quick as a wink she dropped the cookie into Tatty's lap.

When Mrs. Singlittle came into the kitchen Elsie May was standing very sweetly and innocently, with her hands clasped in front of her.

Mrs. Singlittle took the cookie from Tatty's lap and said, "I see you have enough cookies to share with me, my good Charlotte."

Then Mrs. Singlittle broke off a piece of Elsie May's cookie and laid the rest of the cookie back on Tatty's knee.

Cook, coming in the back door, was thinking about preparing vegetables for supper, and did not notice the extra cookie on Tatty's lap. Elsie May watched crossly while Tatty finished her own cookie and then ate what Mrs. Singlittle had left of the second one.

"I wish you would come with me, Charlotte and Elsie May," Mrs. Singlittle said, when she had eaten her piece of cookie and dusted off her fingertips. "I seem to have misplaced my good red fountain pen, and I want someone small and nimble to get around under the tables and chairs in the parlor and have a look."

Tatty swallowed the last of the cookie and got up slowly. Surely Elsie May would find the pen; Elsie May was smarter and faster and would know all the best places to look. Elsie May thought she would find the pen first, too. She held her head high as they followed Mrs. Singlittle to the parlor. A very, very small fire burned (due to Mr. Not So Much's visit) and no lamp was lit. However, it was not yet dusk outside and the girls could see quite well.

"Now look around, my dears," said Mrs. Singlittle. "You, Elsie May, try under the sofa. I was sitting there this afternoon. And you, my good Charlotte, why don't you see if the pen rolled behind the table or under the piano."

Tatty knelt down and looked under the table. Across the room she could see Elsie May kneeling to look under the sofa. Her long yellow braids swung forward and touched the floor.

After Tatty had looked under the table, she crawled over and looked under the piano. There, right in the middle by the pedals, lay the red fountain pen. Tatty could hardly believe her good fortune.

"Here it is, here it is!" she cried, and got up so suddenly that she bumped her head on the piano. But she didn't mind.

"Oh, my good, *good* Charlotte," said Mrs. Singlittle, and gave Tatty a hug and a kiss. Elsie May narrowed her eyes to a squint. Then, to show she didn't care, she tossed her head and went out of the parlor.

Mrs. Singlittle smoothed back Tatty's tousled hair. "How was school today?" she asked. Tatty knew she would have to tell about the spelling paper now. She went out into the hall where she had left her school books. There was the paper. She unfolded it and tried to smooth it out. Oh, why were *her* papers always so wrinkly and smudgy-looking? Mrs. Singlittle would not like *that*.

Slowly she carried the paper into the parlor and gave it to Mrs. Singlittle.

Mrs. Singlittle took the paper and looked at it carefully. Her earrings swung and her eyes glittered. She drew herself up until she seemed to tower over Tatty. Then she said, "Just look at this. Seven words *right*."

She bent forward and gave Tatty a pat on her head. "Seven words right," she repeated. "That's my good Charlotte."

Tatty took her spelling paper and carried it upstairs, wondering what other amazing things would happen that afternoon. Then she heard excited voices as she neared the top of the stairs.

Esmerelda's Second Wish

The voices were coming from Tatty's room, and as she came to the open doorway she could see seven or eight girls gathered around Princess Esmerelda, all talking at once.

Little Ann saw Tatty and squeezed out from the circle around Esmerelda. "Oh, Tatty, guess what Esmerelda has done! She used her second wish. She found Phoebe's button."

The other girls saw Tatty then and began to tell her what had happened, all talking together.

"Phoebe lost a button off her dress—"

"—and she couldn't find it *any*where."

"So Esmerelda was helping, and she said, 'I wish we could find your button, Phoebe.'"

"—and then there it was, right behind the leg of the bed—"

"—right *there*."

Phoebe looked the most excited of all, holding the button up for everyone to see.

"That wasn't a magic wish at all," a voice from the doorway said.

They all turned to see Elsie May standing there, stroking her braids. "And the rain stopping the other day wasn't magic either," she continued. "It was raining all day. It had to stop sometime. And Phoebe was playing right there by the bed this morning. I saw her. The button just came off and rolled under the bed, and there wasn't anything magic about finding it."

All the girls looked back and forth at each other doubtfully. Princess Esmerelda looked confused and a little sad.

"It *was so* magic," said Mary at last. She patted Esmerelda's arm. "Don't pay any attention to her, Esmerelda."

"Yes, it really *was* magic," Phoebe said, holding on to the button tightly so she would not lose it again. She had been afraid Elsie May would tell Mrs. Singlittle she was playing on the floor and ruining her clothes. And then, just when she thought she would never find the button, there it was suddenly right before her eyes. It really was magic to see it there.

"You can believe it's magic if you want to," Elsie May said, sticking up her nose, "but I don't." And she walked away.

A Surprise

One by one the days went by. Cold and gray. Bleak and bare. Windswept and cloud covered.

But there was no snow.

"I can't remember a winter when the first snow was so late," Mrs. Singlittle said.

"Nor can I," Cook agreed.

Every day Esmerelda sat by the window watching, her feet with their satin shoes tucked under her, blue hair falling about her face and shoulders. At night, when she was sleeping in Tatty's bed, she would dream about her castle.

In her dreams she was back there again, walking in her garden, sitting in her throne room, feeding the golden doves in the golden cages that hung from the golden palace walls . . . But in the morning she awoke again surrounded by the noise and chatter of twenty-eight little girls scrambling to be finished with their dressing and bed making in time for breakfast. Then Esmerelda would comb her blue hair and put on her satin shoes and wonder if her enchantment would ever be over. Would it ever?

Every morning twenty-seven girls carried their shoes downstairs to breakfast.

They thought it was marvelous fun, and they slid across the bare, polished hall floor right into the dining room, like skaters on the ice. Elsie May was the only one who did not carry her shoes. She thought it was silly and childish and she was much too dignified for that.

Every day Mr. Not So Much came around to visit. After school, the girls always came in very quietly until they found out whether he was still there or not. If he was in the parlor with Mrs. Singlittle or inspecting Cook's kitchen, the girls spoke in whispers and went outside to play. If he had already gone, things were a little better. Cook would give them something to eat, and they could play what they wanted, and there was nothing more to worry about except a meager supper.

The girls who were supposed to practice piano lessons took turns at the piano. Little Ann stayed out of Cook's way as much as she could, and Phoebe brushed her teeth five times a day so that her chart would have the most checks of all the toothbrush charts when Miss Lavender and Miss Plum returned. All the girls remembered just what Miss Plum had said to them before she left. And they wished she would come back.

Then one day, quite unexpectedly, Esmerelda said, "I think my enchantment is almost over."

"How can you tell? Is it starting to snow?" Everyone in the parlor hurried over to the window where Esmerelda was sitting. A girl named Kate was at the piano practicing, and even she got up and ran over to the parlor window to have a look.

"Why, it's not snowing at all," Kate said with disappointment.

"How can you tell your enchantment is almost over?" Tatty asked.

"I can feel it in my bones," said Esmerelda.

"Like Cook feels when it's going to rain?" Kate said. They had all heard Cook say a thousand times: "It's going to rain. I can feel it in my bones."

"I can feel it in my bones when it's going to be sunny," said Little Ann. But no one was listening to her. They were all straining to see up, up, up into the sky. Each wanted to be the first one to see the first flake falling down.

"How soon do your bones say it's going to happen?" Mary asked.

"Oh . . . soon," Esmerelda answered vaguely. But she seemed satisfied, even though there was not yet actually any snow to be seen.

"Don't tell Elsie May," said Phoebe. "She'll probably lock you up in a closet or something."

"I suppose you'll be happy to get back to your castle," Mary said.

"Who else lives in your castle?" Little Ann asked.

"My mother and father," Esmerelda began, holding up her fingers to count off who lived in her castle.

"Are they the king and queen?" asked Little Ann. She snuggled up beside Esmerelda on the window seat and put her arm through Esmerelda's and her soft little blond head against Esmerelda's shoulder.

"Yes," Esmerelda said, "they are the king and queen. I also have three brothers, but they aren't home all the time. Sometimes they go off to do daring and dangerous things, to fight terrible dragons, to rescue beautiful princesses in distant lands, to win treasures and honors by their brave deeds. They are probably busy right now, searching the countryside trying to find me. Maybe they have captured Old Goblin and are trying this very minute to break my enchantment."

Everyone was silent for a few moments, looking again at the dark winter sky and the bare tree branches.

Then Mary said, "Do you have a sweetheart at home, Esmerelda? A handsome prince, like in the fairy tales?"

Esmerelda smiled. "I have two," she said.

"Two!" said Tatty. Just think, two handsome princes.

"I can't decide between them," said Princess Esmerelda. Her face became very thoughtful and serious. "I must choose one day, of course. When I get back to my castle I will have to try to choose."

"What are they like?" Mary asked.

"One is named Robin. He is very tall and has black hair and black eyes. He is the strongest and bravest prince that has ever lived. Once he led all the armies of our land against a wicked king who had come to conquer us. If it had not been for Robin, we would not have won the battle. The wicked king would be ruling our land."

"Is Robin kind?" asked Tatty. (He sounded a little fearsome to her.)

"Yes, he is very kind," Esmerelda said. "He is kind and wise and brave. He is called Robin the Valiant."

"And what is the other prince like?" asked Mary.

"The other is Prince Michael. He is

called Michael the Fair. His hair is light and curly, and his eyes are green, like the sea. He has sailed to many strange lands and brought back ships full of jewels and spices and silks. He has brought great wealth to my father's kingdom."

"Is he brave and wise and kind, too?"

"Yes," said Princess Esmerelda. "He is brave and wise and kind, too. I love them both—so you see, how can I choose?"

The little girls listened to every word. "I would take Michael," said Phoebe. She thought sailing away to bring home spices and jewels and silks would be the most wonderful life in the world.

"I would take Robin the Valiant," said Kate. She sprang up and pretended to wave a sword.

"Can't you have them both?" asked Little Ann.

"No," said Esmerelda, "I cannot have them both."

"Such nonsense," said Elsie May, who had just come in and seated herself on the piano stool. She twirled herself around once or twice, and the fringe from the cushion stood straight out as she went around.

Tatty was just about to suggest to Esmerelda that her third magic wish could be well used by wishing Elsie May would learn to be nicer—when Phoebe lifted her head and sniffed the air.

"Cook is baking chocolate cake," she cried. Every mouth began to water. They had not had chocolate cake since Miss Lavender and Miss Plum left.

"I'll bet she isn't either," said Kate, after a moment. "We're probably just dreaming it. We haven't had anything good like that since Mr. Not So Much started coming every day."

"But I *smell* it," Phoebe insisted, and the other girls nodded their heads and said, yes, they smelled it, too. Even Esmerelda looked pleased because her friends were going to have chocolate cake.

"I wish we could all have two pieces," Mary said, licking her lips.

"I wish you could, too," said Esmerelda eagerly.

Then everyone stopped chattering and stared at Esmerelda.

"Oh—you've used your third magic wish," Kate said at last. All the girls were silent. They would like to have two pieces of chocolate cake well enough, but it had been fun to think that there was still one magic wish left. Now the wishes were all used up.

"Well, *that* wish won't come true," said Elsie May. "I guess it really would be magic if we got two pieces of anything, the way things are going around here lately."

Just then they heard Mrs. Singlittle coming down the hall from the kitchen. "Ah, here we are," she said, coming into the parlor briskly. How her earrings danced! How her eyes glittered! "Cook's making chocolate cake for dessert tonight," she said. "It is a special occasion: my last night. I thought we ought to have something nice."

"Your last night?" said Elsie May. According to her figures, there were still three more days to go before Miss Plum and Miss Lavender would be coming back.

"Yes, I'm surprised, too," Mrs. Singlittle answered. "A telegram came just a while ago from Miss Lavender and Miss Plum. They have had enough visiting and have decided to come back ahead of time."

"They're coming back! They're coming back!" all the girls began to chant, clapping their hands.

"They should be here sometime tomorrow," Mrs. Singlittle said.

"Why are they coming back early?" Tatty asked. She tugged at Mrs. Singlittle's dress to get her attention. "Aren't they having a good time?" She wanted Miss Lavender and Miss Plum to come—and yet she was afraid of how they might laugh to hear she was "good Charlotte."

"What's that, dear?" said Mrs. Singlittle, who could hardly hear Tatty over all the noise.

"Why are they coming back?" Tatty said again. "Aren't they having a good time?"

"They are having a very good time," Mrs. Singlittle said promptly. She smiled into Tatty's troubled eyes. "They are coming back because they miss you all so much."

"Supper's ready," said Cook, appearing at the parlor door. Mr. Not So Much had made his last tour of *her* kitchen for a while. "There's chocolate cake for dessert," she said with satisfaction. "And two pieces for everybody."

The First Snow

The next day was Saturday, so the girls did not have to go to school. They all had special chores for Saturday morning, and they were all busy when, into the silent, winter-gray day, the first flakes of snow began to fall. It was the first snowfall of the winter.

Tatty was in the kitchen, helping Cook polish silverware. All the shining knives and spoons and forks were lined up in rows on the big round kitchen table. Phoebe was helping, too, pausing often to make silly faces at her reflection in the soup spoons.

"Well, well," said Cook, going to stand by the window. "Here's our first snow."

Tatty and Phoebe let their silverware clatter to the table as they pushed back their chairs and ran to look. There it was indeed, a few sparse, thin flakes growing heavier and steadier even as they watched, until the air was full of white . . . like a feather pillow broken open.

Without even saying an excuse-me-please to Cook, Tatty and Phoebe tore through the kitchen and upstairs to their bedroom, where they had left Esmerelda. She was gone.

Only Mary and Little Ann were in the room.

"Oh, where is she, where is she?" Tatty cried. She could hardly believe their beautiful enchanted princess was gone.

"She was just sitting there by the window one minute, and the next time I looked she wasn't there," Mary said.

"Why weren't you watching to see what happened?" Phoebe scolded. Now they would never know what an enchantment looked like when it was ending.

"I was dusting the bedposts," said Mary.

Dusting was her Saturday-morning chore, and now she felt sad that she had not been watching.

"Why weren't you watching, Little Ann?" Phoebe asked next.

"I was under the bed, hiding from Mary," said Little Ann.

"How could you be hiding from me?" said Mary with much surprise. "I wasn't even looking for you."

"I thought you might start looking for me, if you suddenly didn't see me any-where," said Little Ann. Then she began to cry.

"What is all this commotion?" said Elsie May, who was passing by. But just then they heard someone calling from the hallway below.

"Miss Plum is coming! Miss Lavender is coming!"

The girls almost fell on their heads trying to get downstairs to see.

It was true. The front door stood wide open, and Miss Lavender and Miss Plum

were coming in, the flakes of the first snowfall sprinkled over their shoulders and on their hats. But, oh, they were just the same! They hadn't changed at all—Miss Lavender still about to lose her bouncing hat off her pile of curls; Miss Plum still thin and straight and able to tell in one quick twinkling of an eye that all of the twenty-eight little girls were there, safe and sound, just as she had left them.

Tatty hung back as the other girls crowded around, and Cook came hurrying from the kitchen. Miss Lavender stopped right there in the hall, with her hat and coat and gloves still on, and opened up her suitcase and took out a big paper bag. From the bag she took tiny tissue-wrapped packages and passed them out, one to each girl.

"A little souvenir of our trip," Miss Lavender said. She watched, as excited as the children themselves, as the girls unwrapped their packages.

Some girls found soap carved in the shape of ducks and pigs and cats; some found tiny change purses, just big enough to hold a few dimes and nickels when they went out to find the ice-cream man some summer day; some found pretty pins shaped like bees and frogs and birds; and some found yo-yos that spun down on long white strings.

"What is yours, Tatty?" Miss Plum asked. It had not taken her long to notice that Tatty was hanging back, more quiet for some reason than the other girls.

"A soap pig," said Tatty, holding out the smooth pink pig made of soap.

"Doesn't it smell nice," said Mrs. Singlittle. Tatty smiled at her faintly. Any moment Mrs. Singlittle might call her "good Charlotte"—and then what would she do?

Before long, Miss Lavender and Miss Plum did manage to get off their coats and hats, and everyone went into the parlor. Miss Lavender and Miss Plum sat on the sofa and the girls sat all around, on the floor, on the chairs, and everyplace they could find.

Elsie May ran to get Miss Lavender's gold butterfly brooch from the mantel above the fireplace, where she had put it for safekeeping when Esmerelda gave it to her. "My, my. I was wondering where I lost this," Miss Lavender said.

Then Miss Lavender and Miss Plum answered every question about their trip: about the train ride and the wedding and what the wedding cake tasted like and how much Reginald and his bride liked the silver-dish wedding present . . . . They answered questions such a long while that Mrs. Singlittle had time to go upstairs and finish packing her suitcase. She came down at last, with her suitcase and her coat, and came into the parlor to say good-bye.

"It has been a pleasure," Mrs. Singlittle said to Miss Lavender and Miss Plum. "I have enjoyed all the girls." And then she could not resist adding, "Especially my good Charlotte."

"Good Charlotte?" said Miss Lavender. She looked at Mrs. Singlittle blankly. "Who is that?"

Some of the girls began to giggle. Tatty felt her face grow very warm. Her hands were hot and sticky from holding the soap pig—and she wished she could run away and hide.

Miss Plum was looking at Mrs. Singlittle curiously. "Good Charlotte?" said Miss Plum. "Good Charlotte?"

"Yes, my dear good Charlotte." And Mrs. Singlittle put her arm on Tatty's shoulder and drew her gently forward.

"Oh, you mean *Tatty*," said Miss Lavender. She peered out over the rims of her eyeglasses and nodded wisely.

"This is good Charlotte?" asked Miss Plum. She leaned forward from her seat on the sofa and held out her hand to Tatty. Tatty was very ashamed to give her hand to Miss Plum, for it was sticky and warm and not very clean. Miss Plum did not seem to notice.

"Yes," Miss Plum said, "she is a good girl, indeed. But we didn't know whom you meant. You see, we have always called her Tatty. She is our *good Tatty*."

Tatty was so happy that she did not know what to do. She just stood there, hanging on to Miss Plum with one hand and her pink soap pig with the other. Mrs. Singlittle gave her one last kiss for good-bye, and then she was gone.

"Mrs. Singlittle has holes in her ears,"

Little Ann whispered to Miss Lavender and Miss Plum as soon as Mrs. Singlittle was gone. She had been waiting all these days to tell them.

So, with all the excitement of Miss Lavender and Miss Plum's coming home, Saturday flew by. Tatty and the other girls hardly had time to miss Esmerelda. But that night, when they were in bed, Mary whispered across the room in the darkness, "Well, I guess Esmerelda is in her palace right this minute, trying to decide between Prince Robin and Prince Michael."

"I'd take Prince Michael," said Phoebe, but Kate slept in another room, so she was not there to say she would take Prince Robin.

Outside, the snow that had stopped late in the afternoon began falling again. Softly and silently it drifted down through the night. Down upon Butterfield Square, over the cobblestones and trees and black iron fences. Down upon the rooftops of the old brick houses and against the windows of the little bedroom at Number 18.

"Tomorrow we'll have to wear our shoes to breakfast," Mary reminded anyone who was still awake. Miss Plum never allowed stocking feet.

Well, that was all right, thought Tatty. She wouldn't mind wearing her shoes to breakfast again. Miss Plum and Miss

Lavender were back. Elsie May would have to behave now. And Mr. Not So Much would not be coming every day, so there would be good things to eat. And she was glad to be "Tatty" again. . . .

But Tatty felt that she was going to miss Mrs. Singlittle. She had gotten used to her hugs and kisses, and it really had been amazing the way things had kept turning out right. Tatty remembered it all— shelling the nuts that very first day, finding Mrs. Singlittle's pen under the piano—but before she could think further, Mary spoke again.

"I suppose Esmerelda is sitting in her throne room, wearing her diamonds and her crown and a beautiful silk dress."

Then everything was quiet for a while, and Tatty thought Mary and all the other girls in the room must be asleep. Tatty was very sleepy herself. Sometimes she and Esmerelda had whispered together long after the others were asleep. She missed the girl with the blue hair, but she was glad Esmerelda was safely home. She was glad she had been Esmerelda's friend.

"Is anyone awake?" Tatty whispered.

No one answered.

Outside the snow fell against the window . . . softly . . . softly . . . softly. Tatty snuggled down under her covers. She was happy to be where she was. She was glad Miss Lavender and Miss Plum were home again. It was nice to know they were right downstairs in the parlor, sitting in their chairs by the fire.